Happy 3rd
Birthday, Gavin!
Love,
Mimi & Papa
xoxo

Dear Parents and Educators,

Welcome to Penguin Young Readers! As parents and educators, you know that each child develops at his or her own pace—in terms of speech, critical thinking, and, of course, reading. Penguin Young Readers recognizes this fact. As a result, each Penguin Young Readers book is assigned a traditional easy-to-read level (1–4) as well as a Guided Reading Level (A–P). Both of these systems will help you choose the right book for your child. Please refer to the back of each book for specific leveling information. Penguin Young Readers features esteemed authors and illustrators, stories about favorite characters, fascinating nonfiction, and more!

Go to Bed, Blue

LEVEL **1**

GUIDED READING LEVEL **C**

This book is perfect for an **Emergent Reader** who:
• can read in a left-to-right and top-to-bottom progression;
• can recognize some beginning and ending letter sounds;
• can use picture clues to help tell the story; and
• can understand the basic plot and sequence of simple stories.

Here are some **activities** you can do during and after reading this book:
• Read the Pictures: Use the pictures to tell the story. Have the child go through the book, retelling the story just by looking at the pictures.
• Word Repetition: Reread the story and count how many times you read the following words: *bed, come, look,* and *play.* On a separate sheet of paper, work with the child to write a new sentence for each word.

Remember, sharing the love of reading with a child is the best gift you can give!

—Bonnie Bader, EdM
  Penguin Young Readers program

*Penguin Young Readers are leveled by independent reviewers applying the standards developed by Irene Fountas and Gay Su Pinnell in *Matching Books to Readers: Using Leveled Books in Guided Reading,* Heinemann, 1999.

For Lauren & Allie, who are too old
to be told to go to bed!—BB

To my siblings, Jan, Rick,
Christy, Lisa Ann, and Andy, who all have
special talents of their own—MR

PENGUIN YOUNG READERS
Published by the Penguin Group
Penguin Group (USA) LLC, 375 Hudson Street, New York, New York 10014, USA

USA | Canada | UK | Ireland | Australia | New Zealand | India | South Africa | China

penguin.com
A Penguin Random House Company

Text copyright © 2014 by Bonnie Bader. Illustrations copyright © 2014 by Penguin Group (USA) LLC.
All rights reserved. Published by Penguin Young Readers, an imprint of Penguin Group (USA) LLC,
345 Hudson Street, New York, New York 10014. Manufactured in China.

Library of Congress Cataloging-in-Publication Data is available.

ISBN 978-0-448-48219-4 (pbk)   10 9 8 7 6 5 4 3 2 1
ISBN 978-0-448-48220-0 (hc)   10 9 8 7 6 5 4 3 2

Go to Bed, Blue

by Bonnie Bader
illustrated by Michael Robertson

Penguin Young Readers
An Imprint of Penguin Group (USA) LLC

Look, look.

It is Blue.

Come here.

Come here to play.

We will play.

We will play with Blue.

Look, look.

One, two, three.

Look, look.

One, two, three.

We can jump.

Jump, jump, jump.

Blue is funny.

Come down, Blue.

We can run.

One, two, three.

Blue is funny.

Come here, Blue.

Get to bed, Blue.

No, no.

I want to play.

Look, look.

One, two, three.

We can go up.

Up, up, up.

Stop, stop.

Do not go up.

Come down.

Go to bed, Blue.

Look, look.

One, two, three.

We can play.

No, no.

Go to bed, Blue.

Look, look.

Good night, Blue.